إهداء

لطلابي في نزوى،
آمل أن تتذكروا دائمًا أنكم
جواهر ثمينة

أَنا كَمّة

أنا دائرية،
لوني أزرق،
و شكلي مميز.

يلبسني إلياس،
خاطتني حبوته،
اللي هي أحسن خيّاطة ف
الحارة.

أَنا كُمّة

أنا دائرية،
لوني أخضر،
و شكلي مميز.

يلبسني يوسف،
خاطتني حبوته،
اللي هي أحسن خيّاطة ف الحارة.

أنا دائرية،
لوني أسود،
و شكلي مميز.

يلبسني عمر،
خاطتني حبوته،
اللي هي أحسن
خيّاطة
ف الحارة.

أَنا كمّة

أنا دائرية،
لوني أصفر،
و شكلي مميز،

بس...
ما يعجبني واجد.

يلبسني أحمد بس يا ريت لو يلبسني واحد كبير ولا ذكي ولا قوي.

خاطتني حبوته،
بس كان أحسن لو خاطتني مكينة خياطة،
عشان أسرع وتطلعني كما باقي الكميم مال الناس.

مرّات أحمد يخرب خيوطي
ويخلي فراغات ف زخارفي،
عاد بعدين يلبس مصر عشان
يغطيها.

أنا حبوه.
و أنا أحب أحفادي واجد.
سويت لكل واحد منهم كمة بشكل مميز.

كل كمة تعبر عن
حبي حالهم
بطريقة فريدة.
كل ما شافوا
الناس شغلي،
عرفوا أنا اللي
خطتها.

يا شيبي،
مرّات يخربوا خيوط الكمة و يصير فيها
ثقوب عودة،
و دايمًا يحاولوا يصلحوها بروحهم بس أنا
الوحيدة
اللي تعرف تصلحهن!
يحسبوا إنهم يقدروا يغطوا ثقوب كميمهم
بالمصر،
بس تراه ما يقدروا يقصوا علي، ها!

أعرف كل أحفادي
و أناديهم عشان أصلح كميمهم.
ويديني تعن من كثر الخياطة و التنجيم،
بس من غير شغلي و تعبي كميمهم بتضيع.
كميمهم تطلع احلى كميم و يبين حبي لهم.

المعجم

الكمة:

طاقية دائرية ملونة مطرزة باليد يلبسونها الرجال
كجزء من اللبس العماني التقليدي. مرات تاخذ شهور لين تكتمل و تعتبر هدية مميزة من
حريم العائلة في البيت. التصميم متأثر بالساحل الشرقي في أفريقيا بسبب العلاقة
التاريخية القوية بين أفريقيا و عُمان.

التنجيم:

هي مجموعة من الغرز الصغيرة الي تصنع دائرة أو
"نجمة." تتم حياكتها مع بعض لأشكال ورق الشجر أو الورود و غيرها من
التصميمات العمانية.

المصّر:

قطعة قماشية مطرزة من الصوف مربعة و ملونة و
ملفوفة بعناية حول الكمة بأسلوب العمامة و تكون للمناسبات الخاصة أو الرسمية. تنلف
بطريقة حيث أنها تحمي الأذنين و الرقبة من الشمس.

عُمان:

تقع بين الصحراء الرملية والمياه التجارية، و هي
موطن لأبناء البحر و رواة القصص اللي شافوا الجمال في الثقافات المختلفة لينشروا
تقاليدهم. الملابس العمانية الي تأثرت بشرق أفريقيا و جنوب آسيا والخليج العربي،
عبرت عن ارتباطها العميق بالضيافة و التجارة بين الناس من مختلف
الثقافات على مر الزمان.

Glossary

Kuma:

A round, colorful, hand-embroidered cap that is worn in Oman as part of the national dress by all males. It can sometimes take months to complete and is considered a special gift from female relatives in the home. The design was influenced by the Swahili East African Coast where the Omani people share a strong historical connection.

Massar:

A square embroidered cloth that is neatly wrapped around the Kuma in turban style for special or professional occasions. It is wrapped in a way that protects the ears and neck from the wind, sun, and sand.

Oman:

Nestled between sandy desert and trade waters, this mountainous wonderland is home to sea-farers & storytellers who have found the beauty in different cultures to enrich their own traditions. Influenced by East Africa, South Asia and the Arabian Gulf, Omani clothing expresses its deep connection with hospitality and trade between people of different cultures throughout the centuries.

Tanjeem:

A set of small stitches that make a circle or "star." Many of these are sewn together into leaves, flowers, and other Omani-inspired designs.

I know each grandson and call them over to me so I can fix their kuma. My hands ache from stitching each tiny tanjeem, but without my work, their kuma will fall apart. With my stitches and my love, it becomes the most beautiful kuma ever seen!

Oh, sometimes my grandsons pull at
the threads, and holes start to
appear. They try to fix the holes
themselves,
but only I know how to do that!
They think they can cover up the
holes by wearing the massar on top,
but that doesn't fool me. Ha!

Each design displays my love for them in a unique way. When people see each kuma, they recognize my handiwork.

I am the grandmother.
I love my grandsons.
I made them each a kuma
with its own design.

Sometimes Ahmed makes very big holes in my design by pulling out my stitches. He tries to cover them up by wrapping me in the massar.

I was sewn by his grandmother,
but I wish I was made by machine.
It would make my stitches look like everyone else's.

I am worn by Ahmed,
but I would rather be worn by someone
older, smarter, or stronger.

I am round,
I am yellow,
and I have my own design.
But...
I don't like it very much.

I am a Kuma

I am worn by Omar
and was sewn by
his grandmother,
the best
seamstress in
town.

I am round,
I am black,
and I have my own design.

I am a Kuma

I am worn by Yousef
and was sewn by his grandmother,
the best seamstress in town.

I am round,
I am green,
and I have my own design.

I am a Kuma

I am worn by Elias
and was sewn by his grandmother,
the best seamstress in town.

I am round,
I am blue,
and I have my own design.

I am a Kuma

Dedication

To my students in Nizwa:

May you always remember that you are

masterpieces.

Illustrations and design by Ruth Christiansen
Edited by Michelle Sincock, Kathy Christiansen
Translation by Houriya Mousa, Lamya Alshukeili, Taima Alshukeili, Kendra Sandford, Rgawe, Waffles, Noor,
Amal,and Lexi Al Kharusi
ISBN 978-0-578-61891-3
Printed in the United States of America
10 9 8 7 6 5 4 3 2 1
First Edition

The Kuma
A Wadi Tale

By Julie Christiansen

Illustrated by Ruth Christiansen

Main Translation by Houriya Mousa

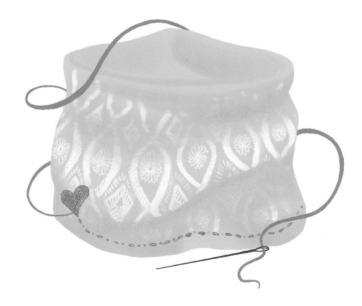